LAW & ORDER

LAW & ORDER

SPECIAL SHAKESPEARE CRIMES

Kathleen Caruso

PALMETTO
P U B L I S H I N G
Charleston, SC
www.PalmettoPublishing.com

Copyright © 2024 by Kathleen Caruso

All rights reserved

No portion of this book may be reproduced, stored in a retrieval system, or transmitted in any form by any means–electronic, mechanical, photocopy, recording, or other–except for brief quotations in printed reviews, without prior permission of the author.

Paperback ISBN: 979-8-8229-3740-6

In the criminal justice system, murder is considered a serious crime. The dedicated Special Shakespeare Squad investigate these vicious felonies and prosecute the offenders without mercy. The members of this coalition are part of an elite squad know as the Special Shakespeare Squad. This is their story.

PROLOGUE

Detective Hamlet is a homicide detective in the Special Shakespeare Squad. He is summoned to a home in Naugatuck, Connecticut on an early Monday morning. The home is owned and occupied by Mr. & Mrs. Macbeth. Over night, Mr. Duncan King, one of two house guests, was brutally murdered. He was stabbed over twenty times in the chest. Mr. Macbeth & Mr. Duncan King have been friends since college, and every year participate together in the civil war re-enactments. Mr. King has two boys and is a huge oil tycoon. Mr. Macduff is a cousin to Mr. Macbeth and is the other guest visiting. Mr. Macduff is going through a divorce because of a drinking problem. This is their story....

ACT 1

Scene 1.
[Crime Scene, occupied by officers and medical examiner]
Enter Detective Hamlet

Detective Hamlet *Observes the body.* Angels and ministers of grace defend us. *To medical examiner Lennox*: What's the matter?

M.E. Lennox Strange screams of death

Detective Hamlet Sir, a whole history.

M.E. Lennox The night has been unruly. Those of of the house it seems had done 't. Their hands and faces were all badged with blood.

Exit medical examiner

Detective Hamlet I am glad to see you well Horatio-- or I do forget myself.

Detective Horatio The same.

Detective Hamlet What's his weapon.

Officer Osric Rapier and dagger.

Detective Hamlet Whose was it?

Officer Banquo Macbeth.

Detective Horatio Season your admiration for a while with an attent ear till I may deliver upon the witness[es].

Detective Hamlet Go on, I'll follow thee.

Exit Detective Hamlet and Officer Horatio

Scene 2.
[A room with the first witness]
Enter Detective Hamlet and Officer Horatio

Detective Hamlet	Good even sir . Who is this ?
Mr. Macduff	Macduff.
Detective Hamlet	Art thou a truepenny?
Mr. Macduff	I am not treacherous.
Detective Hamlet	Come, give a taste of your quality.
Mr. Macduff	I would not be the villain thou think'st for the whole space that's in the tyrants grasp. Great tyranny lay thou thy basis, for goodness dare not check thee: wear thee thy wrongs; the title is affeered.
Detective Hamlet	Who?
Mr. Macduff	Not in the legions of horrid hell can come a devil more damned in evils to top.
Detective Hamlet	I humbly thank you. God by to you.

Exit Officer Horatio and Detective Hamlet. They walk.

Detective Hamlet	*To Horatio*: Tears in his eyes, distraction in his aspect, a broken voice. What, ho Horatio?
Detective Horatio	I did very well note him.
Detective Hamlet	Ay, sir what of him?

Detective Horatio   Now cracks a noble heart. Heaven
                    will direct it each word made true
                    and good.
                    Exit Detective Hamlet and Detective Horatio

Scene 3.
[A room with the suspects Mr. & Mrs. Macbeth]
Enter Detective Hamlet and Detective Horatio

Detective Hamlet   Good even sir, How is it with
                    you lady? *Detective Hamlet
                    bows. Looking at Mr. Macbeth he
                    continues.* Who is this?
Mr. Macbeth   My name's Macbeth.
Lady Macbeth   What's the business?
Detective Hamlet   Murder.
Mr. Macbeth   When?
Decective Horatio   Yester night.
Detective Hamlet   Did you see nothing? Nor did you
                    nothing hear?
Mr. Macbeth   Who's there? What ho?
Detective Hamlet   What?
Mr. Macbeth   Had I three ears, I'd hear thee.
Detective Hamlet   What, I do not well understand
                    that!
Mr. Macbeth   I have a strange infirmity. Give
                    me your favor, my dull brain was
                    wrought with things forgotten.

	Kind gentlemen your pains are registered where every day I turn the leaf to read them.
Detective Hamlet	There are no sallets in your lines to make the matter savory, nor no matter in the phrase that might indict the author of affection , but called it an honest method, as wholesome as sweet and by very much more handsome than fine.
Mr. Macbeth	What is't you say?
Detective Hamlet	There is a kind of confession in your looks, which your modesties have not craft enough to color, confess yourself to heaven , repent what's past, avoid what's to come.
Mr. Macbeth	What is't you say ? I do repent of me my Fury. Avuant! And quit thy sight! Let the earth hide thee! Thy bones are marrowless, thy blood is cold; thou has no speculation in those eyes which thou dost glare with.
Detective Hamlet	Come, come, deal justly with me. Come, come; nay speak.
Mr. Macbeth	Thou canst say I did it. You make me Strange even to the disposition that I owe. We will proceed no further in this business.

Detective Horatio	Stay! Speak, speak. I charge thee speak.
Detective Hamlet	I'll have thee speak out the rest of this soon. Do you hear?
Mr. Macbeth	They have tied me to a stake; I cannot fly, but bear like I must fight the course. What's he that was not born of women? Such a one am I to fear of one.
Lady Macbeth	I pray you, speak not! He grows worse and worse; questions enrage him; at once good night.
Detective Hamlet	Rest, rest perturbed spirit. *Quit room Detectives Hamlet and Horatio*
Detective Hamlet	*To Officer Horatio:* Is it not monstrous that this player here but in a fiction in a dream of passion could force his soul to his own conceit? Such an act it is not madness but mad in craft.

ACT 2

Scene 1. [District Attorney Lear's office]
Enter Detective Hamlet and Detective Horatio

Detective Hamlet	How is it with you?
D. A Lear	How dost thou? What wouldst thou with us?
Detective Hamlet	Murder. A bloody deed, I will tell you why. Monday morning murder done for his estate.
D.A. Lear	Five days we do allot thee for provision to come betwixt our sentence.
Detective Hamlet	Is't possible?
D.A. Lear	It shall be done, I will arraign them. Go get it ready, nothing can be made out of nothing.
Detective Hamlet	*Looks excitedly at his partner Horatio.* Excellent.

Scene 2.
[Police Station interview room
with Lady Macbeth nervously fidgeting in a chair.]
Enter Detective Hamlet

Detective Hamlet	*To Lady Macbeth*: I have news to tell you. Murder, though it have no tongue, will speak.
Lady Macbeth	What do you mean?

Detective Hamlet	You jig and amble and you lisp; you make your wantonness your ignorance.
Lady Macbeth	A foolish thought and all-thing unbecoming.
Detective Hamlet	Look here upon this picture. *Violently Slams a picture down in front of Lady Macbeth.* Look you how pale he glares. Have you eyes? Eyes without feeling, feeling without sight, ears without hands or eyes, smelling sans all!
Lady Macbeth	Thou'rt mad to say it.
Detective Hamlet	I'll no more on' t, it hath made me mad. You mouth it trippingly on the tongue. Why, look you there *pointing to the picture.*
Lady Macbeth	Help me hence, ho! *She attempts to rise and leave the interview.*
Detective Hamlet	Sit you down and let me wring your heart, for so I shall if it be made of penetrable stuff.
Lady Macbeth	NO more o ' that now more o' that. Woe, alas. *Lays down her head and cries uncontrollably.*

Exit Detective Hamlet

Scene 3
[Police Station, interview room with Mr. Macbeth waiting inside]

Mr. Macbeth	What man dare approach thou like the rugged Russian Bear, The armed rhinoceros, or th' Hyrcan tiger, Take any shape but that and my firm nerves shall never tremble. False face must hide what the false heart doth know.

Enter Detective Hamlet

Mr. Macbeth	Well then now have you considered of my speeches? In our last conference; passed in probation with you our innocent self.
Detective Hamlet	How if I answer no? Your news is not true. Let me question more in particular.
Mr. Macbeth	Why, what care I?
Detective Hamlet	So oft it chances in particular men that for some vicious mole of nature in then as in their birth where in thy are not guilty by the O'ergrowth of some complexion oft breaking down the pales forts of reason or by some habit that too much o'erleavens the form of applausive manners that their

	virtues else by be they as pure as grace, infinite as man may undergo, shall in the general censure take corruption from that particular fault. The dram of evil doth all noble substance of a doubt to his own scandal.
Mr. Macbeth	Ay, in the catalogue ye go from men. I require clearness.
Detective Hamlet	Why?
Mr. Macbeth	I have but golden opinions from all sorts of people.
Detective Hamlet	Nay, I have an eye of you. A murderer and a villain.
Mr. Macbeth	A false creation. I have no spur to prick the sides of my intent.
Detective Hamlet	How now? Dead for a ducat am I not I'th'right?
Mr. Macbeth	*Smiles maliciously.* I am a prosperous gentleman.
Detective Hamlet	Indeed. Your ladyship would do the motive and cue for passion.
Mr. Macbeth	*Noticeably pales and begins to shake his leg in agitation.* Thou speak'st false.
Detective Hamlet	*Noticing Mr. Macbeth's agitation continues:* Your ladyship calls virtue hypocrite and sets a blister there, makes marriage vows as false as

	dicers' oaths. The power of beauty will sooner transform honesty from what it is to a bawn.
Mr. Macbeth	*Mr. Macbeth growls.* Upon the next tree shalt thou hang alive thou lily-livered boy. Take thy face hence.
Detective Hamlet	Rebellious hell in a matron's bones when the compulsive ardor gives the charge since frost itself as actively doth burn, and reason panders will. O such a deed as from the body of contraction plucks the very soul.
Mr. Macbeth	Say, from whence you owe this strange intelligence?
Detective Hamlet	Your ladyship. She well instructs me.
Mr. Macbeth	*Shouts* Liar!
Detective Hamlet	I do not think so. Not this, by no means. In the rank sweat of an enseamed bed, stewed in corruption, honeying and making love over the nasty sty--
	Mr. Macbeth violently jumps up yelling Cutting off Detective Hamlet..
Mr. Macbeth	Accursed by that tongue that tells me so.
	Detective Hamlet jumps up and shouts.

Detective Hamlet I'll lug the guts into the neighbor room. Your ladyship lapsed in time and passion, let the bloat King tempt her to bed, pinch wanton on her cheek, call her his mouse, and let him for a pair of reechy kisses , or paddling in her neck with his damned fingers.

Mr. Macbeth sags back into his chair with a look of defeat.

Mr. Macbeth That suggestion whose horrid image doth unfix my hair and make my seated heart knock at my ribs. I am sick at heart. Death of thy soul.

Detective Hamlet walks over to Mr. Macbeth
To stand behind him. He leans over
And speaks softly.

Detective Hamlet The man that is not passion's slave, whose blood and judgment are so well commeddled, I take to be a soul of great rareness. Wilt thou hear now how I did proceed why the man dies? The trappings and the suits of woe I most powerfully and potently believe been struck so to the soul by the heartache and the thousand natural shocks the lady he loved well a strumpet.

Mr. Macbeth	O full of scorpions in my mind. I have done the deed Duncan is in his grave . My dearest love should have died.

ACT 3

Scene 1
[District Attorney Lear's Office]
Enter District Attorney Lear, Detectives Hamlet & Horatio
And Assistant District Attorney Portia

D.A. Lear	Know that we have divided all cares and business, conferring them on younger strengths.
Detective Hamlet	*To District Attorney Lear:* Ay sir. *To Assistant District Attorney Portia:* How is it with you lady?
A.D.A. Portia	I am informed thoroughly of the cause.
Detective Hamlet	What did you enact? With all his crimes broad blown he here proclaims madness.
A.D.A. Portia	The brain may devise laws for the blood, but a hot temper leaps o'er'a cold decree, but this reasoning is not in the fashion I may choose nor refuse. I'll have that doctor speak.
Detective Hamlet	Without more circumstance at all I hold it fit that we shake hands and part. Farewell.
A.D.A. Portia	Peace be with you.
D.A. Lear	Peace.

Exit Detective Hamlet

Scene 2

[Assistant District Attorney Portia's Office]
Enter Assistant District Attorney Portia,
District Attorney Lear and
Forensic Psychiatrist

A.D.A. Portia	What mercy can you render him?
Doctor	I have two nights watched but can perceive no truth in your reports. I doubt not of his temperance.
D.A. Lear	*To A.D.A. Portia:* Consider him well.
Doctor	Good night.
	Exit Doctor
A.D.A. Portia	What dost thou say?
D.A. Lear	My poor fool is hanged! In our courtwe'll go I'th'morning.
	Exit All

# ACT 4

Scene 1
[Court Room]

A.D.A. Portia	*To the jury*: Of these events at full, let us go in and charge us there upon inter gatories and we will answer all things faithfully.
	Mr. Macbeth is called to the stand.
A.D.A. Portia	*To Mr. Macbeth*: A quarrel solely led by nice direction of a maiden's eyes. How all the other passions fleet to air and rash embrace mingled with the husbandry green-eyed jealousy. Is this true?
Mr. Macbeth	Who can be neutral in a moment? No man, the expedition of my violent love outrun the pauser reason.
A.D.A. Portia	Be advised to these injunctions before you hazard the state of hellish cruelty with an unquiet soul. But what of your wife being the bosom lover of your dear friend?
Mr. Macbeth	A friend? I see thee still proceeding from the heat-oppressed brain. My dear wife *he laughs to himself*, the filthy hag.
A.D.A. Portia	Speak not so grossly! In your account the ruin of your love

	commits itself to be directed from your friend. To pay the debt you must cut flesh from off his breast twenty times over.
Mr. Macbeth	His gashed stabs are less than horrible imaginings.
A.D.A. Portia	Do you confess?
Mr.Macbeth	Life's but a walking shadow, a poor player that struts and prets his hour upon the stage and then is heard no more. It is a tale told by an idiot, full of sound and fury signifying nothing. I will not be afraid of death.
A.D.A. Portia	Then confess!
Mr.Macbeth	The gracious Duncan have I murdered.
A.D.A. Portia	*To the jury:* Though justice be thy plea, consider this, that in the course of justice none of us should see salvation.

Exit Jurors

Scene 2
[Court Room]
Enter Jurors

Foremen Angelo   We must not make a scarce crow
of the law, setting it up to fear the
birds of prey, and let it keep one
shape, till custom make it their
perch and not their terror. The jury,
the sworn twelve have passing on
the prisoner's life. He must die.

THE END

CITATIONS

[1] Detectives Hamlet & Horatio, Officers Osric and Banquo
[2] Mr. & Mrs. Macbeth's, Macduff, Medical Examiner Lennox
[3] District Attorney Lear
[4] Assistant District Attorney Portia
[5] Forensic Psychiatrist
[6] Forensic Psychiatrist
[7] Foreman Angelo

---

[1] Shakespeare, William. Hamlet. Signet Classics, 1998
[2] Shakespeare, William. Macbeth. Signet Classics, 1998
[3] Shakespeare, William. King Lear. Signet Classics, 1998..
[4] Shakespeare, William. Merchant of Venice. Signet Classics, 1998.
[5] Shakespeare, William. Macbeth. Signet Classics, 1998.
[6] Shakespeare, William. King Lear. Signet Classics, 1998.
[7] Shakespeare, William. Measure for Measure. Signet Classics, 1998.

www.ingramcontent.com/pod-product-compliance
Lightning Source LLC
LaVergne TN
LVHW092101060526
838201LV00047B/1520